W9-AYK-266

Dear Parent:
Your child's love of reading starts here!

Every child learns to read in a different way and at his or her own speed. Some go back and forth between reading levels and read favorite books again and again. Others read through each level in order. You can help your young reader improve and become more confident by encouraging his or her own interests and abilities. From books your child reads with you to the first books he or she reads alone, there are I Can Read Books for every stage of reading:

SHARED READING
Basic language, word repetition, and whimsical illustrations, ideal for sharing with your emergent reader

BEGINNING READING
Short sentences, familiar words, and simple concepts for children eager to read on their own

READING WITH HELP
Engaging stories, longer sentences, and language play for developing readers

READING ALONE
Complex plots, challenging vocabulary, and high-interest topics for the independent reader

ADVANCED READING
Short paragraphs, chapters, and exciting themes for the perfect bridge to chapter books

I Can Read Books have introduced children to the joy of reading since 1957. Featuring award-winning authors and illustrators and a fabulous cast of beloved characters, I Can Read Books set the standard for beginning readers.

A lifetime of discovery begins with the magical words "I Can Read!"

Visit www.icanread.com for information
on enriching your child's reading experience.

To Jacob D. and Jacob B.,
two lesser-known
but fearsome pirates
of the Caribbean
—J.S. and P.C.

I Can Read Book® is a trademark of HarperCollins Publishers.

Library of Congress Cataloging-in-Publication Data is available.
ISBN 978-0-06-143519-5 (trade bdg.) — ISBN 978-0-06-143521-8 (pbk.)

11 12 13 14 15   SCP   10 9 8 7 6 5 4 3 2 1 ❖   First Edition

I Can Read!

READING WITH HELP 2

NEVER KICK A GHOST

AND OTHER SILLY CHILLERS

BY JUDY SIERRA
PICTURES BY PASCALE CONSTANTIN

HARPER
An Imprint of HarperCollinsPublishers

Contents

1. THE SKELETON BRIDE   6

2. I'M NOT SCARED OF WITCHES: 15

     A HAND-CLAPPING RHYME

3. NEVER KICK A GHOST   16

4. HERE LIES THE BODY . . .   20

5. THE BIG SLOBBERY MONSTER   22

     Where the Stories Come From   32

The Skeleton Bride

One fine day,
Blackbeard the Pirate
and South Sea Sue
were married on
Blackbeard's ship.

After the wedding, Sue asked,

"Why don't we play a game?"

"Hide-and-seek!"

yelled the pirate crew.

"I'll hide first," said Sue.

"Cover your eyes."

Sue found a big wooden chest
and she got inside.
The lid shut
and the lock snapped.

The pirates looked high and low,
but they didn't look
in the big wooden chest.

Boom! Boom! Cannons fired.

The pirate ship was under attack.

Blackbeard and his crew got away,

but the ship sank to the bottom.

No one saw South Sea Sue again
for a hundred years.

One day, a diver found

a big wooden chest

at the bottom of the sea.

The diver opened the rusty lock.

The diver lifted the lid and saw

the long white dress,

the long white bones,

and the smiling face

of Blackbeard's skeleton bride.

I'm Not Scared of Witches: A Hand-Clapping Rhyme

I'm not scared of witches.

I'm not scared of bears.

I'm not scared of hungry monsters

underneath the stairs.

Never Kick a Ghost

Sam Sniff was a mean, mean man.

One night, Sam took a walk

in the old graveyard.

He saw something white

and as big as a possum.

Sam kicked it.

It changed into something
as big as a hog.
Sam kicked it.

It changed into something
as big as a cow.
Sam kicked it.

It turned into something so big,

it scared Sam out of his mind.

Sam ran all the way home.

He said four words before he died:

"Never kick a ghost."

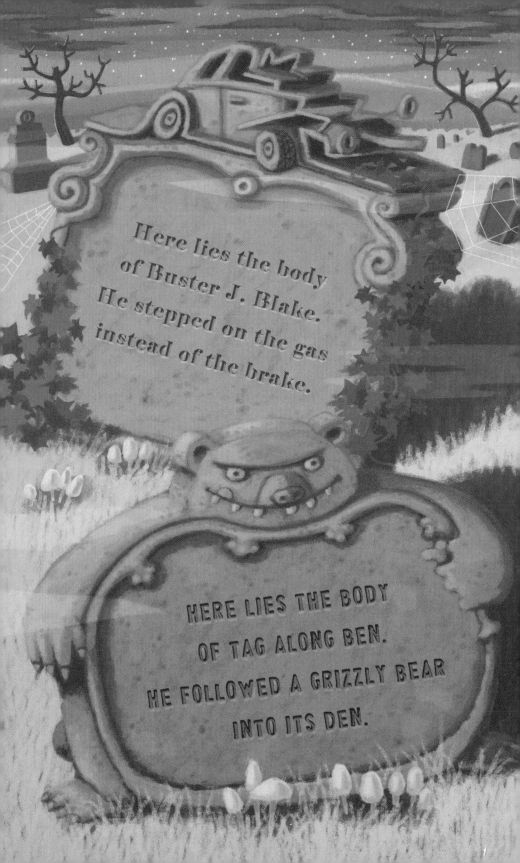

Here lies the body
of Buster J. Blake.
He stepped on the gas
instead of the brake.

HERE LIES THE BODY
OF TAG ALONG BEN.
HE FOLLOWED A GRIZZLY BEAR
INTO ITS DEN.

HERE LIES THE BODY
OF ANNA, OUR SISTER.
SHE WAS JUST FINE UNTIL
DRACULA KISSED HER.

The Big Slobbery Monster

One rainy day as I was on my way home,
I heard footsteps behind me.

Slowly I turned.

I saw a big slobbery monster.

The monster had long green fingers
and floppy purple lips.
He smiled at me and said,
"Look what I can do
with my long green fingers
and my floppy purple lips."

I screamed, *"Aah!"*

I ran until I had to stop

to catch my breath.

Slowly I turned.

I saw that big slobbery monster
with long green fingers
and floppy purple lips.

He winked at me and said,
"Look what I can do
with my long green fingers
and my floppy purple lips."

I screamed louder. *"Aaaaah!"*

I ran home as fast as I could.

I went into my bedroom.

I locked the door.

Slowly I turned.

I saw that big slobbery monster
with long green fingers
and floppy purple lips.

"All right!" I shouted.
"Show me what you can do
with your long green fingers
and your floppy purple lips."

The big slobbery monster
put his long green fingers
on his floppy purple lips.

Blub-blub-a! Blub-blub-a! Blub-blub-a!

WHERE THE STORIES COME FROM

"The Skeleton Bride" is based on an old English ghost story found, among other places, in *Folktales of England*, edited by Katharine M. Briggs and Ruth L. Tongue. University of Chicago Press, 1965, p. 88.

"I'm Not Scared of Witches" is a playground rhyme collected by the author in 2007 from elementary school students in Berkeley, California.

"Never Kick a Ghost" is adapted from "The Ghost on the Cemetery Road" in *The Frank C. Brown Collection of North Carolina Folklore*, edited by Newman Ivey White. Duke University Press, 1952–64, vol. 1, p. 675.

"Here Lies the Body . . ." is adapted from classic joking epitaphs.

"The Big Slobbery Monster" is the author's version of a ghost story parody.